What Does It Look Like?

Alice Jednik

INFOMAX
COMMON CORE
READERS

Rosen Classroom™

New York

Published in 2013 by The Rosen Publishing Group, Inc.
29 East 21st Street, New York, NY 10010

Book Design: Katelyn Londino

Photo Credits: Cover Alexey Rozhanovsky/Shutterstock.com; p. 4 Jin Young Lee/Shutterstock.com; p. 5 auremar/
Shutterstock.com; p. 6 Stuart Elflett/Shutterstock.com; p. 7 Keith Bell/Shutterstock.com; p. 8 littleny/Shutterstock.com;
p. 9 © iStockphoto.com/glass-eye-studios; p. 10 © iStockphoto.com/Matt_Brown; p. 11 Johann Helgason/
Shutterstock.com; pp. 12, 16 (hula hoop) © iStockphoto.com/frankoppermann; pp. 13, 16 (blocks) Nenov Brothers
Photography/Shutterstock.com; p. 14 © iStockphoto.com/Neustockimages.

ISBN: 978-1-4488-8974-7
6-pack ISBN: 978-1-4488-8975-4

Manufactured in the United States of America

CPSIA Compliance Information: Batch #WS12RC: For further information contact Rosen Publishing, New York, New York at 1-800-237-9932.

Word Count: 141

Contents

I like going to the toy store
with my friends.
We see lots of fun toys!

Ethan likes the toy cars.

This toy car is red.

What color is this toy car?

This toy car is blue.

What color is this toy car?

This toy car is yellow.

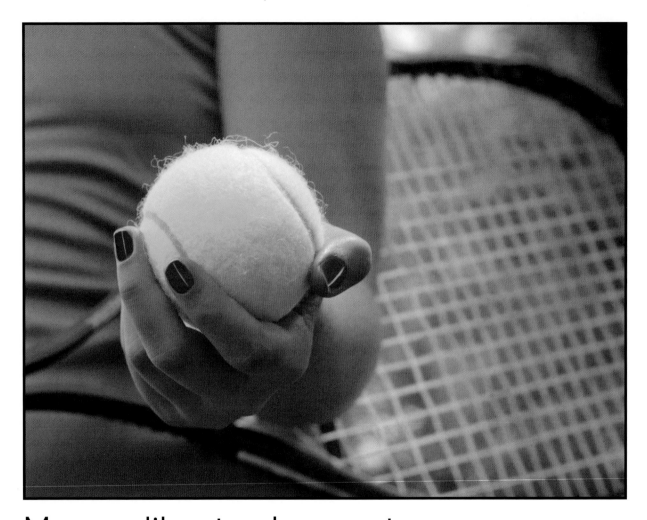

Morgan likes to play sports.

She finds a tennis ball.

The tennis ball is small.

Morgan finds a softball.

It's bigger than the tennis ball.

Morgan finds a basketball.

It's the biggest ball in the store!

Josh finds a kite.

The kite is shaped like a diamond.

Emily finds a hula hoop.

The hula hoop is shaped like a circle.

I find some blocks.

The blocks are shaped

like squares and rectangles.

We had a great time at the store!

What would you get at the toy store?

What does it look like?

Describing Words

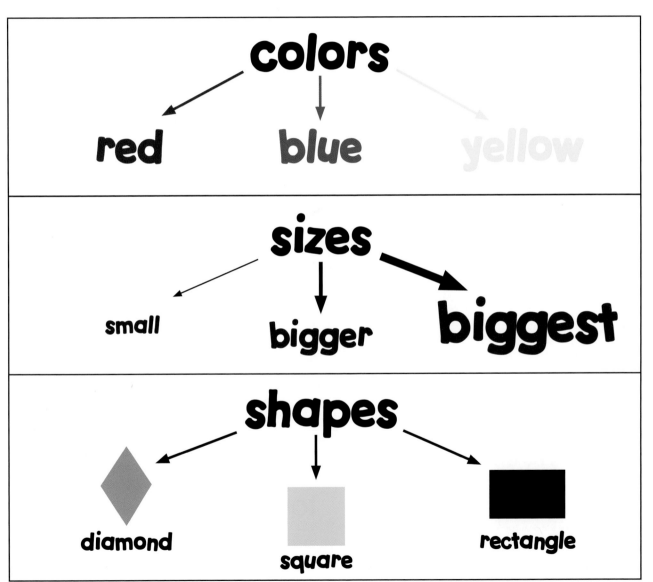

colors
- red
- blue
- yellow

sizes
- small
- bigger
- biggest

shapes
- diamond
- square
- rectangle

Words to Know

blocks

diamond

hula hoop

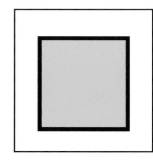

square

Index